Let's Share, Grumpy Bunny!®

For Bud Rogers for sharing his friendship and his berries
—J.K.F.

For Sophia May, who always shares . . .
—Lots of love, Lucy

Text copyright © 2006 by Justine Korman Fontes.
Illustrations copyright © 2006 by Lucinda McQueen.

All rights reserved. Published by Scholastic Inc.
SCHOLASTIC, CARTWHEEL BOOKS, GRUMPY BUNNY,
and associated logos are trademarks
and/or registered trademarks of Scholastic Inc.
Lexile is a registered trademark of MetaMetrics, Inc.

ISBN-13: 978-0-439-87383-3
ISBN-10: 0-439-87383-5
10 9 8 7 6 5 4 3 2 1   9 10 11 12 13/0

Printed in the U.S.A.
This edition first printing, September 2009

Let's Share, Grumpy Bunny!

by Justine Korman Fontes
Illustrated by Lucinda McQueen

Cartwheel
·B·O·O·K·S·®

SCHOLASTIC INC.

New York   Toronto   London   Auckland   Sydney
Mexico City   New Delhi   Hong Kong   Buenos Aires

Chapter 1
Seeing Red

Hopper O'Hare loved art class.
But he didn't like sharing paints.
Everyone always wanted to use the
same color.

Hopper reached for the blue paint.
So did Lilac.
The cup spilled!
"Worms!" Hopper said.
"I'm sorry," Lilac said.

Everyone always forgot to wash
the brushes.

"You got red in the yellow!" Hopper
yelled at Marigold.

"I'm sorry," Marigold said.

The art teacher talked to Hopper.
"You are a very good artist," Mrs.
Violet said. "But you have to learn
to share."
Hopper sighed. "Wiggly worms!"
he said.

"Would you like to paint a poster?"
Mrs. Violet asked Hopper.

Hopper's ears flew up.
He clapped his paws.

"You will work with Corny,"
Mrs. Violet added.
Hopper's ears flopped down.
"But, I…"
"This is your chance to share,"
Mrs. Violet said.
Hopper grumbled.

Chapter 2
Hey, You, Get Out
of My Blue!

Hopper wanted to paint the poster.
So he had to share.
The boys decided to paint a big
meadow.

But they kept bumping into each other.
Hopper tried moving.
Corny's elbows were everywhere!

Corny painted the tree trunk.
"That's my tree!" Hopper said.
Corny splashed brown paint on
Hopper's nose.
"Sorry," he said.

Hopper painted green grass.
"That looks like fun!" Corny said.
Corny painted green grass, too.
"I think I'll add some red and blue
flowers," he said.

He dipped his brush into the cup.
Uh-oh!

Chapter 3
Purple Power

Corny forgot to wash his brush.
The sky had a red swirl in it!
Hopper was so angry!
His ears turned as red as the paint.
"Wiggly worms on toast!" Hopper yelled.
"You got red paint in the blue!"
"I'm sorry," Corny said.

Hopper looked at the poster.
Getting angry won't help, he thought.
Hopper calmed down by counting to ten.
Just then, Hopper saw a purple swirl.
He had an idea!

Hopper took an empty paint cup.
He poured in a little red and a little blue.
He mixed them until he had purple.
"Let's add a purple monster to our meadow!" Hopper said.
"That's a great idea!" Corny said.
"The Great Grape Googly-Moogly!" Hopper shouted.

The boys painted a big, purple monster.
It was fun!

Chapter 4
The Great Grape
Googly-Moogly

Hopper and Corny kept painting.
They did not fight.
"I'm so glad we added the monster,"
Corny said. "The meadow was boring
without him."

Mrs. Violet came over to check
their work.

"He's a wonderful monster," she said.
"The Great Grape Googly-Moogly!"
the boys shouted together.

Mrs. Violet hung up the poster.
"I'm very proud of you, Hopper,"
Mrs. Violet said.

"You calmed down and solved your problem. You both painted a great poster. And you did it by sharing."

Hopper felt very proud and happy.
Now he would share everything.
Sharing was a lot of fun!